THE ZACK FILES

Great-Grandpa's in the Litter Box

For Judith, and for the real Zack,
with love—D.G.

THE ZACK FILES™

Great-Grandpa's in the Litter Box

By Dan Greenburg

Illustrated by Jack E. Davis

GROSSET & DUNLAP • NEW YORK

I'd like to thank my editors,
Jane O'Connor and Judy Donnelly,
who make the process of writing and revising
so much fun, and without whom
these books would not exist.

I also want to thank
Jennifer Dussling and Laura Driscoll
for their terrific ideas.

Text copyright © 1996 by Dan Greenburg. Illustrations copyright © 1996 by Jack E. Davis. All rights reserved. Published by Grosset & Dunlap, Inc., a member of Penguin Putnam Books for Young Readers, New York. THE ZACK FILES is a trademark of The Putnam & Grosset Group. GROSSET & DUNLAP is a trademark of Grosset & Dunlap, Inc. Published simultaneously in Canada. Printed in the U.S.A.

Library of Congress Cataloging-in-Publication Data
Greenburg, Dan.
    Great-Grandpa's in the litter box / by Dan Greenburg ; illustrated by Jack E. Davis.
      p.   cm. — (The Zack files)
    Summary: Zack takes home from the local animal shelter a scruffy tomcat who not only talks but claims to be the reincarnation of Zack's Great-Grandpa Julius.
    [1. Cats—Fiction. 2. Reincarnation—Fiction. 3. Great-grandfathers—Fiction.
    4. Supernatural—Fiction.]   I. Davis, Jack E., ill. II. Title. III. Series: Greenburg, Dan. Zack files.
PZ7.G8278Gr 1996
[Fic]—dc20   96-7117
                                                    CIP
                                                    AC

ISBN   0-448-41260-8   I J

Chapter 1

My name is Zack. I'm ten years old and I guess you could say I've been interested in weird stuff all my life. Stuff like haunted houses, UFOs, and storms where it rains frogs. So when something weird happened to me, I was probably more open-minded than somebody else who wasn't interested in weird stuff all their life.

I was in the animal shelter near our home in New York City. After years of begging my dad for a cat, he finally broke down and said yes. I could get a kitten. So here I was.

I passed a cage with an old gray tomcat inside it. His fur was matted with dirt. He'd lost half the whiskers on the left side of his face, which made him look a little lopsided. And the tip had been chewed off of one of his ears.

"Sssst! Young man!" Someone was calling me. The voice sounded raspy and strange. "Hello, little boy! Over here!"

I turned around, looking to see who it was. But there was nobody in sight.

I went on to a cage where a little tuxedo kitten with a black body and white paws was taking a nap. He sure was cute. I stopped to take a closer look at him. Of course, it probably wasn't the best time for me to adopt a kitten. In a couple of days my dad and I were flying to Chicago to spend Thanksgiving with my Grandma Leah. But our neighbor had agreed to cat-sit. And I wasn't taking any chances of my dad changing his mind.

I'd almost decided on that cute little tuxedo kitten when I heard the voice again:

"Hey, kid," said the voice. "I am *speaking* to you."

"Where are you?" I asked.

"Right here, dummy," said the voice. "In the cage in back of you."

I turned around. That scruffy old gray tomcat was staring quite crossly at me.

"You'll pardon me for hollering," said the cat. "But I was afraid you were about to make a terrible mistake and choose somebody else."

"You can *talk*!" I said, hardly able to believe my ears.

I moved closer to his cage. I wanted to see if his cat lips moved when he talked. Maybe this was just a trick—somebody doing ventriloquism. I mean I told you I like weird stuff, but this was really far out, even for me. "A talking cat?" I said.

"Yeah, a talking cat, how about that," said the cat sarcastically.

His cat lips were moving! This was no trick!

"But look at you—a talking boy," he said. "Listen, we don't have much time. You've got to get me out of here."

"What do you mean?"

"I mean I can't stand it in here a minute longer," he said. "The meowing and the

smell are driving me right up the wall. Tell them you're adopting me."

"Uh, I don't mean to hurt your feelings," I said. "But I've already decided on this little tuxedo kitten here." Like I said before, I'm pretty open-minded. I had nothing against talking cats. I just wasn't sure I wanted to live with one. Especially with one as bossy as this one seemed.

"The tuxedo kitten?" he said. "Poor choice."

"What do you mean?"

"He has fleas and worms. Plus he never got the hang of using a litter box."

The tomcat gave me a long look. He could see I wasn't buying it.

"OK," the cat went on. "I didn't want to have to use this. But here goes: If you don't adopt me, they're going to put me to sleep.

And I don't mean tuck me in bed in my jammies either. I mean kill me. You really want that on your conscience, kid?"

"Listen, they don't put cats to sleep here," I said. "That is a well-known fact." This cat was not only bossy, he also seemed to have problems with the truth.

"OK, I admit they haven't lately," he said. "But that could change any day."

I looked at him and shook my head.

"OK, OK," he said. "How's about this: What if I told you I know your name?"

"What's my name?"

"Zack."

"How—how did you know that?" I asked. I had to admit I was pretty impressed. Not that many people know my name, and even fewer cats.

"You're impressed, huh?" said the big

gray tomcat. "What if I told you I'm a member of your family, Zack? Do you think you'd still prefer the little tuxedo?"

"A member of my *family*?" I said. "How could that be? You're a cat."

"Hey, you never heard of reincarnation? Somebody dies and comes back as somebody else?"

"So?" I said. Sure, I'd heard of reincarnation. In fact, I'd read about several cases in India of kids who claimed to have lived before. They knew facts about certain places they'd never been, things they couldn't possibly have known if they were ordinary kids. Still, they were kids, not cats. "So what?"

"So," said the gray tomcat, "I happen to be your wonderful dead Great-Grandfather Julius."

Chapter 2

One minute I'm about to go home with a cute little black-and-white kitten, the next a big gray tomcat tells me he's my dead great-grandfather. I didn't know what to do. I took another look at the kitten. He was licking his front paw in an adorable way. The tomcat saw I was still leaning toward the kitten.

"What? You don't think I'm cute?" he asked. Then he posed in what he must have thought was a cute pose.

"You're...*kind* of cute, sir," I said. "It's just that..."

"Cute, shmute," he said. "You can't tell me you're going to walk out of here with a flea-bitten stranger who hasn't been properly toilet-trained and leave your beloved great-grandfather rotting in a stinking little cage? Family is family, Zack."

I looked at the tomcat, then at the kitten, then at the tomcat. *Family is family*. Funny, that's something Grandma Leah always says. That did it.

"I guess you're right, sir," I said. "I guess family is family."

"Now you're talking sense, kid," said the cat. "And, please, call me Great-Grandpa Julius."

Chapter 3

When I arrived home, huffing and puffing, carrying my cardboard cat carrier, my dad met me at the door. Since my parents split up, I live part of the time with my dad and part with my mom.

"So," he said, smiling, "it looks like you've finally gotten yourself a kitty."

"Yeah," I said, and put the cat carrier down. I was exhausted. With Great-Grandpa Julius inside it, it must have weighed close to thirty pounds.

"Can I see the little guy?" asked my dad.

"Sure, Dad," I said. "But first I have to tell you a couple of things."

"OK, what?"

"Well, number one, I didn't get a kitten. I got a slightly older cat."

"Why, Zack," said my dad, "I think that's a wonderful thing to do, giving an older cat a home. I'm very proud of you, son."

"Uh-huh. And number two, he's not an ordinary cat, Dad. He's...well, for one thing, he talks."

"He talks," said my dad.

"Yeah, he talks."

My dad smiled, deciding to go along with my little joke.

"I see. Well, what does he say?"

"He says he's Great-Grandpa Julius."

"I didn't even think you remembered having a Great-Grandpa Julius," he said, chuckling.

What I remembered was hearing Grandma Leah go on about her father, Julius, who was so nice he was practically a saint. Then she'd always add how Julius was the complete opposite of Great-Grandpa Maurice, her husband's father. Maurice was the black sheep of the family.

So far, Julius didn't seem that saintly to me. I opened the cat carrier. Great-Grandpa Julius and my dad took a good long look at each other.

"Well, he's certainly...big," said my dad. "Hello, Great-Grandpa Julius. Remember me? Dan? You always used to say I was your favorite grandchild. Can you say hello?"

Great-Grandpa Julius seemed about to say something. Then he scratched behind his ear with his hind leg instead.

"He's not very talkative," said my dad.

"You should have heard him at the animal shelter," I said.

My dad chuckled and walked off, shaking his head.

"How come you didn't talk to my dad?" I asked.

"I talk when I want to," said the cat, "not when other people want me to. Hey, Zack, you got anything to eat around here? I'm so hungry I could eat rodents."

I had the free can of cat food they gave me at the animal shelter. I put it into a bowl on the floor. Great-Grandpa Julius sniffed it and wrinkled up his nose.

"Feh!" he said. "What *is* that stuff?"

"Beef by-products in gravy," I replied.

"You got maybe a little herring with sour cream?"

I told him we didn't have anything like that. He did not take this at all well.

"Let's put it this way, kid," said Great-Grandpa Julius. "Either get me some herring with sour cream pronto, or I'm going to take a leak on your sofa."

"You're not serious about this," I said.

"Try me," he said.

If you ask me, Great-Grandpa Julius was a lot crankier than I'd heard. But I was trying to be understanding. I guess dying and getting reincarnated as a cat could spoil a person's mood.

Chapter 4

Luckily, the deli on the corner sold herring with sour cream. I brought it back to Great-Grandpa Julius.

"Now you're talking," he said when he saw it. He gobbled it up. "Not bad. Not bad at all. But tomorrow, Zack, be sure the deli man doesn't skimp on the sour cream."

Boy, this cat was pushy!

"Listen, I can't buy you herring and sour cream every day," I said. "I only get three dollars a week allowance. And I won't be able to buy it for you over Thanksgiving weekend—I won't even be here. I'm going to Chicago. To visit Grandma Leah."

"We're going to visit Leah?" he asked delightedly.

"*I* am," I said. "You're staying here with a neighbor."

"You'd go to Chicago and you wouldn't take me to see my own daughter? If Leah heard I was reincarnated and didn't come to see her, she'd be crushed."

"Well," I said, "let me ask my dad."

~⌐~

"Zack," said my dad, "I'm willing to go along with a joke. But we both know cats can't talk. Although I must admit I'm tempted to bring him to Chicago, just to see the expression on Grandma Leah's face when you tell her that cat is her father."

"Dad, I'd really like to take him to Chicago. I think it would mean a lot to him."

"I'll tell you what," said my dad. "If you can get him to talk to me, you can take him to Chicago."

I went back to my room, where Great-Grandpa Julius was pawing through my collection of baseball cards.

"You have any cards with Lou Gehrig, Ty Cobb, or Rogers Hornsby on them?" he asked.

"No, I'm afraid not."

"Gehrig and Hornsby were nice fellas. Cobb not so nice."

"That's what I hear."

"But all three signed my baseball."

"You're saying you actually met Lou Gehrig, Ty Cobb, and Rogers Hornsby?" I said. The tomcat nodded. "What happened to the ball they signed?"

"I have it."

"Where?"

"In a safe place, don't worry about it. So did your dad say I could come to Chicago?"

"He said on one condition."

"What's that?"

"You have to talk to him. I don't think he believes you can talk."

"That's all I have to do, talk to him?"

"That's all."

"OK, let's do it."

I followed Great-Grandpa Julius, who padded into the living room, where my dad was reading the newspaper.

"Dad," I said, "Great-Grandpa Julius has something to say to you."

"Really?" said my dad. He put down his

paper and turned toward the cat, with a big smile on his face. "All right," he said. "Tell me. What was the hardest part about changing from a person into a cat?"

Great-Grandpa Julius looked at my dad a moment without speaking. Then he cocked his head, opened his mouth, and said, "For me, I guess the hardest part was finding out there wasn't a door you could lock behind you on the litter box. Is that good enough for a trip to Chicago?"

My dad's eyes looked like they were going to pop right out of his head.

"Sounds good enough to me," I said. "How about you, Dad?"

Chapter 5

Once my dad found out my cat was Great-Grandpa Julius, he kept asking him questions about what it was like being dead. Dad never let up for the two days before we left for Chicago, and all during the long ride to the airport.

"Some people who died and were brought back to life again claim they went through what looked like a very long tunnel with very bright light at the other end,"

said my dad. "And all their dead relatives met them on the other side. Did that happen to you?"

"I do remember going through a long tunnel and coming out to bright light on the other side," said Great-Grandpa Julius.

"You do?" said my dad excitedly.

"Yes," said Great-Grandpa Julius. "It happened to be the Midtown Tunnel. And the bright light on the other side was Queens. That's where they buried me. Tell me something. Would you happen to have a cigar on you? It's been years since I've smoked a really good cigar."

"You should stop smoking cigars," I said. "They're bad for you."

"I guess you're right," said Great-Grandpa Julius. "But some things you just don't stop craving, even after you're dead."

"How long have you been a cat?" asked my dad.

"I don't have a driver's license on me," said Great-Grandpa Julius. "How old do I look?"

"About twelve or thirteen," I said.

"That feels about right," he said. "Of course, I didn't come back as a cat right away."

"You didn't?"

"Oh no. First I was a caterpillar."

"A caterpillar?" I said. "What was that like?"

"Extremely boring. Mostly it was about eating leaves. I ate leaves and tried to pretend they were herring with sour cream. Say, you wouldn't by any chance happen to have a little schnapps on you?"

"What's schnapps?" I asked.

"Liquor," said my dad. "No, I'm sorry, I don't carry schnapps on me."

We arrived at the airport. Dad paid the cab driver. I tried to put Great-Grandpa Julius back into his cat carrier.

"Hey, c'mon," he cried. "Don't make me travel in a suitcase again. I'm a dignified old geezer, for Pete's sake."

"In a past life you were a dignified old geezer," I said. "In *this* life you're a stray cat. And cats travel in cat carriers."

Julius sighed and got into his carrier.

Once we got on the plane, Dad started in again with his questions.

"So, Julius," said Dad, "after you were a caterpillar, did you become a butterfly?"

"No, a moth," said the voice inside the cat carrier. "Mostly that was about eating sweaters."

"You ate sweaters?" I said. "Ugh!"

"Don't knock it till you've tried it," said Great-Grandpa Julius. "I remember one fine cashmere turtleneck. It was almost as tasty as a corned beef on rye. Then one night I happened to fly a little too close to a torch outside a Polynesian restaurant and—pffft!"

"Another tunnel?"

"No, no, moths don't get tunnels. Only humans get tunnels. After that I became a mouse."

"And that was all about eating cheese, I suppose," said my dad.

"No, about eating wood. Don't ask."

"Wait a minute," I said. "First you were a caterpillar, then you were a moth, then a mouse. How did you have time to be all those things?"

"We're not talking about a lot of time here," said Great-Grandpa Julius. "You could die, do a stretch as a caterpillar, then a moth, then a mouse, and you could still be back by a week from Thursday. But time didn't matter to me. I was dead. I had quite a lot of leisure time on my hands."

"Excuse me," said the flight attendant as she passed our row. "In preparation for takeoff, please make sure your seat belts are securely fastened and that your seat backs and tray tables are in the upright and locked position."

"Hey, cookie," said Great-Grandpa Julius, "what are you doing after the flight?"

The flight attendant thought my dad said that, because she gave him a dirty look.

Then we buckled up. Next stop—Chicago!

Chapter
6

"Before we see her, I just want to ask you one thing," said my dad in the elevator of the building on Lake Shore Drive where Grandma Leah lives.

"What's that?" I asked.

"Grandma Leah is in her eighties. Do you really think it's safe to tell a woman in her eighties that her dead father is now a cat?"

"Grandma Leah is a very peppy, open-minded person," I replied. "I'm sure she'll take the news OK."

The elevator doors opened on the seventh floor and we walked down the hall to Grandma Leah's apartment, my dad carrying our luggage and me carrying the carrier with Great-Grandpa Julius in it.

Grandma Leah was so happy to see us. She kept hugging and kissing us all over the place. When we were all settled in her apartment she noticed the cat carrier for the first time.

"Don't tell me you brought an animal all the way to Chicago?" she said.

"Not just any animal, Grandma," I said. "A very special animal."

"Special in what way?" asked Grandma Leah.

"Special in the way that he is not only a cat, he is also a member of our family," I said.

"In other words, you love him so much you feel he's a member of our family?" asked Grandma Leah.

I looked at my dad and then back at Grandma Leah.

"No," I said, "I mean he really is a member of our family."

And with that I opened up the cat carrier. Grandma Leah and Great-Grandpa Julius took their first look at each other.

"Grandma Leah," I said, "I believe this is your father, Great-Grandpa Julius."

Grandma Leah stared at the cat in silence for a moment and then shook her head.

"No," she said. "I don't believe it is. My father was taller."

"Leah dear," said Great-Grandpa Julius, "it's so wonderful to see you again. How have you been all these years, my darling?"

"It's talking to me," said Grandma Leah in a very strange voice. "A cat is talking to me in the English language."

"He is," I said.

"Leah dear," said Great-Grandpa Julius, "I may be a cat, but I'm also your father."

"It's still talking to me," said Grandma Leah. "Am I right about this, that the cat is still talking to me?"

"You're right," I said.

"Tell the cat I said it's not my father," she said.

"Why don't you tell him yourself?" I suggested.

"I don't talk to cats," said Grandma Leah in the same strange voice.

"Grandma Leah says you're not her father," I said.

"I *heard* her, I *heard* her," said Great-Grandpa Julius. "What am I, deaf?" Then the cat softened his voice. "Leah dear, don't you remember me? It's Daddy!"

"Tell the cat I said that we never called my father by the name of Daddy," said Grandma Leah. "Ask it what we called my real father."

"She says what name did she call you?" I asked.

"I heard her, I heard her." Great-Grandpa Julius's voice was rising. "You don't have to repeat everything she says."

"Well then, what name did she call you?"

"It wasn't Daddy," said Great-Grandpa Julius.

"We've already heard her say it wasn't Daddy," said my dad.

"Of course it wasn't Daddy," said Great-Grandpa Julius. "Because it was... Father."

Grandma Leah shook her head.

"Tell the cat it wasn't Father," said Grandma Leah.

"She says it wasn't—"

"*Don't repeat it!*" snapped Great-Grandpa Julius angrily. Then he quickly recovered his composure. "It wasn't Father. Of course it wasn't Father," he said. "Father was what I called myself. What you called me was...Papa."

"Tell the cat it wasn't Papa," said Grandma Leah.

"Oh boy," said Great-Grandpa Julius.

"Could I ever use a good cigar or a glass of schnapps right about now. Leah dear, I'm over a hundred years old. I've been a caterpillar, a moth, a mouse. I've died many times, so my memory isn't quite what it used to be. Could you please give me a break here and tell me what you used to call me?"

"Go on, Grandma Leah," I said. "Tell him what you used to call him."

"I didn't call the *cat* anything," she said. "I called my *father*—my real father, my human father—Poppy."

"Poppy, shmoppy," said Great-Grandpa Julius. He waved his paw dismissively. "How far is Poppy from Papa?"

"Wait a minute," said Grandma Leah. "I just realized something."

"What's that?" I said.

"Did the cat say it wanted a good cigar or a glass of schnapps?"

"That's what he said," I said.

"My father, Julius, never smoked cigars. And he never drank schnapps. You know who smoked cigars and drank schnapps?"

"Who?" I said.

"Who?" said my dad.

"The black sheep of the family, that's who. Your cat is a liar, Zack. He's not my father, Julius, at all. He's your grandpa's no-good father. He's Great-Grandpa Maurice!"

Chapter 7

"Is what Grandma Leah says true?" I demanded of the large gray tomcat. "Are you my grandpa's no-good father, Maurice?"

"Now, hold your horses, sonny, hold your horses," he said. "First of all, where does she get off calling me a no-good?"

"Where do I get off?" said Grandma Leah angrily. "I'll tell you where I get off. You took thirty thousand dollars of my father's money to work on your crazy inventions. Then you left town. Disappeared. We never heard a word from you again."

We all turned to the cat.

"What inventions?" I asked.

"I'll tell you what inventions," said Grandma Leah. "A hairpiece for bald eagles was one."

"Who would ever buy a hairpiece for bald eagles?" I asked the cat.

"Well, that was a problem," said the cat.

"Then there was the dog whistle," Grandma Leah went on. "Only dogs were supposed to be able to hear it."

"That sounds better," I said.

"Except for one little thing," she said. The cat looked embarrassed. "Dogs could not hear it either. You blew it and all the mice in the neighborhood came running."

"Did you invent anything that worked?" I asked.

"Yes!" said the cat. "A sweater for dachshunds in the shape of a hot dog bun. Very cute, if I do say so myself. At first it didn't sell. I thought I'd lost all of Julius's money, so I beat it out of town. But you know what? After a while that sweater started selling like crazy. Everybody who owned a dachshund had to have one. I made back the whole thirty thousand. I had it sent directly to a secret bank account in Chicago."

"A secret bank account?" I said.

"In the Morton F. Acropolis Savings and Loan Association of Chicago," said the cat. "I was coming to Chicago to pay Julius back when I got hit by a Greyhound bus."

We all stared at the cat.

"Great-Grandpa Maurice," I said gently. "You've told us many things that weren't true. How do we know what you're telling us now is the truth?"

"First thing tomorrow morning," he said, "take me to the Morton F. Acropolis Savings and Loan Association of Chicago. Then you'll find out."

Chapter 8

And so the next morning, right after breakfast, my dad, my Grandma Leah, my Great-Grandpa Maurice, and I all got into a cab and went to the Morton F. Acropolis Savings and Loan Association of Chicago.

At first the bank officer we spoke with told us she couldn't find any secret bank account bearing the number Maurice had given us.

"Tell her to look harder," said Maurice from inside the cat carrier.

The bank officer looked startled.

"Please look harder, ma'am," I said.

And so the bank officer looked harder.

"You'd better be telling us the truth about this," I said to the cat carrier.

"Don't be so mistrustful," said the voice from inside the cat carrier.

The bank officer returned.

"I did find something," she said. "An account was opened a great many years ago. I don't know if it's the right one. But it does bear the same number you gave me."

"What's the name on the account?" I asked.

"That, of course, would be a secret," said the bank officer.

"What if I told you the first name?" I said. "Would you just nod your head if I'm right?"

45

"What name are you thinking of?" she asked.

"Maurice," I said.

The bank officer nodded.

"I'm right!" I said. Great-Grandpa Maurice was telling the truth! "Now how do we get the money?"

"Well, the individual whose name is on the account would have to sign for it," she said.

We all looked at each other.

"What if he couldn't do that?" asked my dad.

"Why couldn't he do that?" said the bank officer.

"What if he were...What if something had happened to him?" I said.

"Such as what?" said the bank officer.

"Such as, oh, I don't know, such as he

turned into a cat," I said.

"Such as he *died*," said my dad quickly.

"Well, if the account holder is deceased," said the bank officer, "then the money would go into probate. Probate is a very long, very complicated legal process. It takes years to sort out."

"What does deceased mean?" I whispered.

"Dead," said the voice inside the cat carrier.

"What if he turned into a cat?" I asked.

"Excuse me?" said the bank officer.

My dad looked at me and shook his head.

"Do you believe in reincarnation?" I asked the bank officer.

"No," she said.

We all looked at each other. We didn't

have any idea what to do next.

"Hey," said the voice in the cat carrier, "can I talk to her?"

"Is there somebody inside that animal carrier?" asked the bank officer, alarmed.

"Hey, let me out of here!" said the voice.

I looked at my dad. He shrugged. I opened the cat carrier. Great-Grandpa Maurice hopped out onto the counter.

"Uh, I'm afraid pets aren't allowed inside the bank," said the bank officer, "The regulations specifically forbid— "

"Oh, pipe down a minute, sis," said Great-Grandpa Maurice. "And maybe we can clear this up."

The bank officer looked like she might faint.

"This," I said, "is my great-grandfather, Maurice. He opened the account with your bank many years ago when he was still a person."

The bank officer leaned heavily against the counter so she wouldn't fall down.

"This individual does, indeed, appear to be...a cat," she whispered.

"You're darned tootin' I am," said Great-Grandpa Maurice. "And if you don't mind, I'd like to withdraw all the money in my account and give it to my family."

"Are you able to...sign for it?" she whispered, barely able to speak.

"Hey, dollface," he said, "I'm a cat. Maybe you noticed. I don't happen to have an opposable thumb. So I can't hold a pen."

"If you're unable to sign," she whispered, "we would be unable to...give you the money."

"Why the heck not?" he asked.

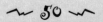

"It would not be...consistent with company policy," she whispered, her eyes now squeezed shut.

"Then how's about changing company policy?" he said. "From now on, anytime somebody gets reincarnated as a cat and comes in to get his money, all he has to do is ask for it. What do you say?"

The bank officer took a deep breath.

"I just don't...know if we can do that," she said.

"OK then, get me Morty," said Great-Grandpa Maurice.

"Who's Morty?" asked the bank officer.

"Who's Morty?" repeated Great-Grandpa Maurice. "You mean to say you don't know Morton F. Acropolis, the founder of the bank?"

And with that, the cat leapt off the

counter and hotfooted it down the hall.

"Now just a minute there," the bank officer called after him. "I can't let you— "

Great-Grandpa Maurice stopped in front of a fancy door. It said "Morton F. Acropolis" on the front.

"Hey, Morty!" yelled Great-Grandpa Maurice. "You in there?"

"Maurice?" called a surprised voice from inside the office. "Maurice, is that you?"

The cat pushed the founder's door open with his nose and walked inside. My dad, Grandma Leah, and I followed close behind. The bank officer came right after us.

Behind a long desk that looked like some kind of antique sat the oldest man I had ever seen. He was also one of the shortest.

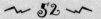

I doubt if he was a lot taller than me, and he had on a pair of glasses with amazingly thick lenses.

"Hey, Morty, great to see you!" said the cat.

"Maurice, you old dog, is that you?" cried Mr. Acropolis. He squinted through his glasses and peered over the top of his desk. "My eyes aren't what they used to be. But I'd recognize that voice anywhere, even after all these years!"

"So how have you been, Morty?"

"Never mind me, what about you, Maurice? I heard you were dead."

"I was," said the cat. "But I'm better now. Listen, Morty, I got a problem. Maybe you can help me."

"For you, Maurice? Anything. What can I do?"

"Sir," said the bank officer, "do you realize you're talking to a c—"

"Quiet, Lola," snapped the old man. "I haven't seen this man in ages."

"But he's not a man, sir," said the bank officer, "he's a c—"

"Quiet!" shouted Mr. Acropolis. "Go ahead, Maurice, what can I do for you?"

"It's the money I made on the hot dog sweater, Morty. I'd like to withdraw it from my account. But this young lady here tells me I can't."

"Poppycock!" roared Mr. Acropolis. "I invested in that hot dog sweater myself. Smartest move I ever made. Give the man his money, Lola!"

"But, Mr. Acropolis, he's unable to sign for it."

"Why's that?"

"He can't hold a pen in his paws," she said.

"Well, I can't hold a pen in *my* paws either," said Mr. Acropolis. "A man gets to be our age, dear, there are certain things he can't do by himself any longer. Help him, for the love of Pete!"

"Y-yes, sir," said the bank officer.

And so we all walked out of Mr. Acropolis's office. Then, with shaking hands, the bank officer put a pen between the cat's paws and helped him sign his name. Then she wrote out a check and handed it to us. My dad looked at the amount and whistled.

"Maurice, I thought you said there was thirty thousand dollars in this account," he said.

"How much is in there?" asked Maurice.

"Closer to ninety," said my dad.

"Ninety thousand dollars?" asked Grandma Leah. It was the first thing she'd said since we'd arrived at the bank.

"Well, that's after more than thirty years of interest," said my dad.

"And you really want us to have this?" I asked.

"On one condition," said Maurice.

"What's that?"

"That you leave me enough for a first-class, one-way ticket to Palm Beach, and a few years' rent in a deluxe pet hotel, with a standing order for herring and sour cream every morning, and a glass of schnapps every night."

"You're not going to live with us?" I said.

"As much as I love you, Zack," said Maurice, "I've always wanted to spend my golden years in Florida. I understand there are folks down there who might be willing to invest a few dollars in inventions of a somewhat speculative nature."

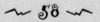

So Maurice went off to live the good life in Florida. But before he did he had the bank officer open his safe-deposit box. There it was. A baseball signed by Lou Gehrig, Ty Cobb, and Rogers Hornsby.

"This is for you, kid," he said to me. "I was going to keep it, but hey, what the heck does an old pussycat need with an old baseball anyway?"

Even though Great-Grandpa Maurice was kind of pushy, I was really sad to see him go.

"Hey, Zack," he said, "cheer up. Now you can go back to the animal shelter and

get that little tuxedo kitten you were looking at."

"But you said he has fleas and worms
and never learned how to use a litter box,"
I replied.

"Maybe so," he said. "But there's one
thing about him that might make you over-
look all that."

"What?"

"In a former life he was Babe Ruth."

What else happens to Zack?

Find out in

ZAP! I'm a
Mind Reader

Lightning must have knocked out the power. I was pretty freaked out, alone in the dark science room.

Carefully I got up from my desk. From the flashes of lightning, I could almost see well enough to get to the door.

When I was about halfway there, I got this really creepy feeling. The feeling that I wasn't alone in the room. And right after that, I picked up a thought. It said, *There he is! Now I have him! The time to kill is now!*